This book belongs to:

....

....

Editor: Ruth Symons
Designer: Bianca Lucas
Managing Editor: Victoria Garrard
Design Manager: Anna Lubecka

Copyright © QED Publishing 2013

First published in the UK in 2013 by
QED Publishing
A Quarto Group company
230 City Road
London EC1V 2TT

www.qed-publishing.co.uk

A catalogue record for this book is available from the British Library.

ISBN 978 1 78171 133 0

Printed in China

I'm the
HAPPIEST

Anna Shuttlewood

QED Publishing

It was a beautiful sunny day, and all the animals were gathered together. Giraffe had his head high in the trees.

"I'm the **tallest**," said Giraffe. "And being tall is the most useful thing in all the world."

The other animals

s t r e t c h e d

as high as they could ...

But none of the other animals
could stretch as high as Giraffe.
They didn't like that Giraffe
was the tallest.

Only Raccoon was happy for Giraffe.

"Oh, you are very tall," he said.
"You must be a hundred times
taller than me. I'm so happy
that you are tall."

Raccoon started **jumping**

and **clapping** his hands

and dancing his **happiest** dance.

"Well, I'm the **spikiest**," said Hedgehog.
"Spikes keep me safe from danger and make me pretty."

None of the animals were
spiky, and it made them jealous.
Only Raccoon was happy for Hedgehog.

"Yes, you are spiky and pretty," said Raccoon. "No one is as spiky as you are. It makes me want to dance my **happiest** dance."

"Pretty?!" squealed Pig. "Pretty means to be nice and round. I am the prettiest."

"Colour is important, not shape," said Frog.
"I am green, and green is the best colour.

The grass is green...

... the trees are green...

... no one is greener than me!"

The other animals
were not green like
Frog, and they grumbled.
Only Raccoon was **happy** for Frog.

The animals all started to boast that *they* were the best.

"I can jump the **highest**."

"I'm the **stripiest**."

"I'm the most **colourful**."

"I'm the **spottiest**."

"I'm happy that Giraffe is tall, Hedgehog is spiky, Pig is round and Frog is green," said Raccoon.

"You're all so wonderful and different —
it makes me want to dance my **happiest** dance!"

Raccoon danced around,
twirling and **leaping**.
It was such fun, it made all
the other animals happy too!

"I'm happy that
Mouse is **small**
and Elephant is **big**...

... I'm happy that Snake is **long** and Leopard is *spotty*."

They all danced the happiest dance —
but Raccoon was happiest of all.

"I'M THE HAPPIEST!"

Next steps

Show the children the cover again. Could they have guessed what the story is about from looking at the cover?

This book features lots of different animals from all over the world. Can the children spot an animal from Africa? Can they spot an animal from the Arctic? Ask the children if they have ever been to a zoo. Which animal did they like the most and why? Have they got a favourite animal?

Try playing the following game. Ask the children to think of an animal and use just one word that best describes it. The rest of the group should then guess what the animal is.

Discuss the story with the children. Explain to them that everyone is different but that we're all equally important. Ask the children how they would describe themselves in one word. What feature are they most proud of?

Ask the children if they like hearing about other people's good qualities and achievements. Have they ever been jealous of a friend or family member because they did well at something? Explain to the children that it's important to appreciate other people's qualities.

Ask the children why they think Raccoon is so happy. What makes the children happy?